The curious tale of Fi - Rex!

Jamie and Jools Oliver, Amanda Holden, Ronan Keating, Bear Grylls,
Rod Stewart and Penny Lancaster, Coleen and Wayne Rooney, Denise Van Outen,
Andy Murray, Keith Lemon, Tom Daley, Sir Paul McCartney, One Direction, Take That,
Kate Moss, Annabelle Neilson, Nick Grimshaw and Kylie Minogue.

The Land of Your Imagination →

First published in 2015 by Fat Fox Books Ltd.
www.fatfoxbooks.com

ISBN: 978-1910884003

Fat Fox and associated logos are trademarks and/or registered
trademarks of Fat Fox Books Ltd.

A CIP catalogue record for this book is available from the British Library.

Printed and bound in Slovenia.

The curious tale of
Fi - Rex!

All profits donated to BBC Children in Need

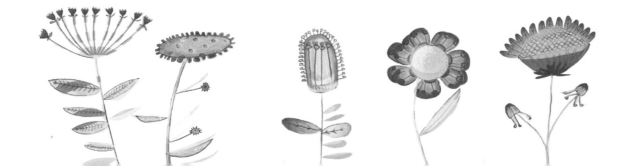

n a bright summer's day, on a green-grassed farm, stood a small cottage. The morning sun shone through a bedroom window onto a girl's face, waking her to start the day. But this was no ordinary girl, and today would be no ordinary day. This was Fi-Rex, half-girl, half-dinosaur.

Ten years ago, when Fi (as she was known then) was just a baby, she found a magic, glowing fossil on the beach. From the moment she touched it, the bottom half of Fi turned into a magnificent dinosaur.

Far from bothering Fi-Rex, being half a dinosaur definitely had its advantages! The alarm clock rang loudly and with a quick swish of her tail she switched it off. Fi-Rex had been dreaming of cakes. Snuggling back under the covers, she was just returning to her scrumptious thoughts, when there was a knock at her bedroom door.

"Wake up, sleepy scales!" shouted a little boy's voice. "Mum says I'm not allowed to open my presents until you come downstairs." It was Fi-Rex's little brother, Max. It was his seventh birthday today and that meant the whole family was going to a theme park.

Jamie and Jools Oliver

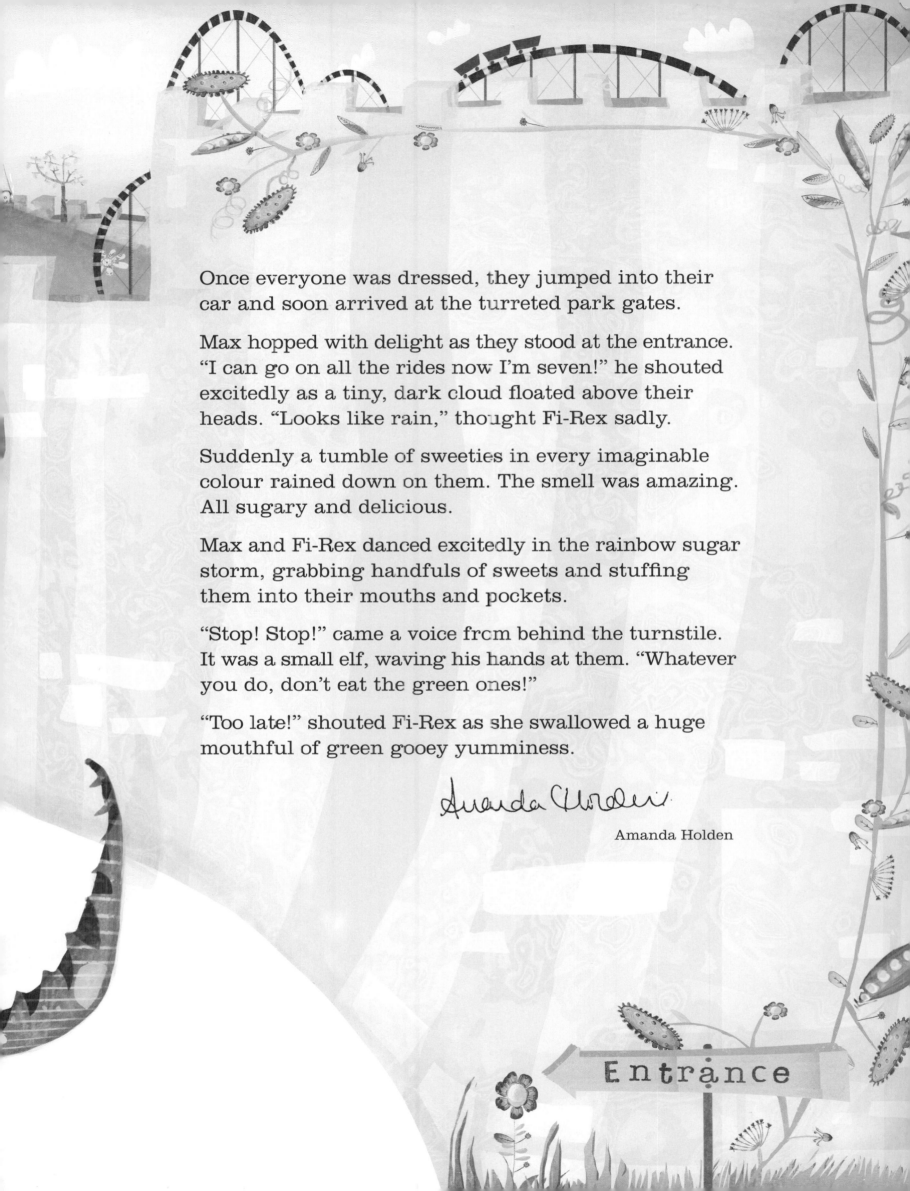

Once everyone was dressed, they jumped into their car and soon arrived at the turreted park gates.

Max hopped with delight as they stood at the entrance. "I can go on all the rides now I'm seven!" he shouted excitedly as a tiny, dark cloud floated above their heads. "Looks like rain," thought Fi-Rex sadly.

Suddenly a tumble of sweeties in every imaginable colour rained down on them. The smell was amazing. All sugary and delicious.

Max and Fi-Rex danced excitedly in the rainbow sugar storm, grabbing handfuls of sweets and stuffing them into their mouths and pockets.

"Stop! Stop!" came a voice from behind the turnstile. It was a small elf, waving his hands at them. "Whatever you do, don't eat the green ones!"

"Too late!" shouted Fi-Rex as she swallowed a huge mouthful of green gooey yumminess.

Amanda Holden

Entrance

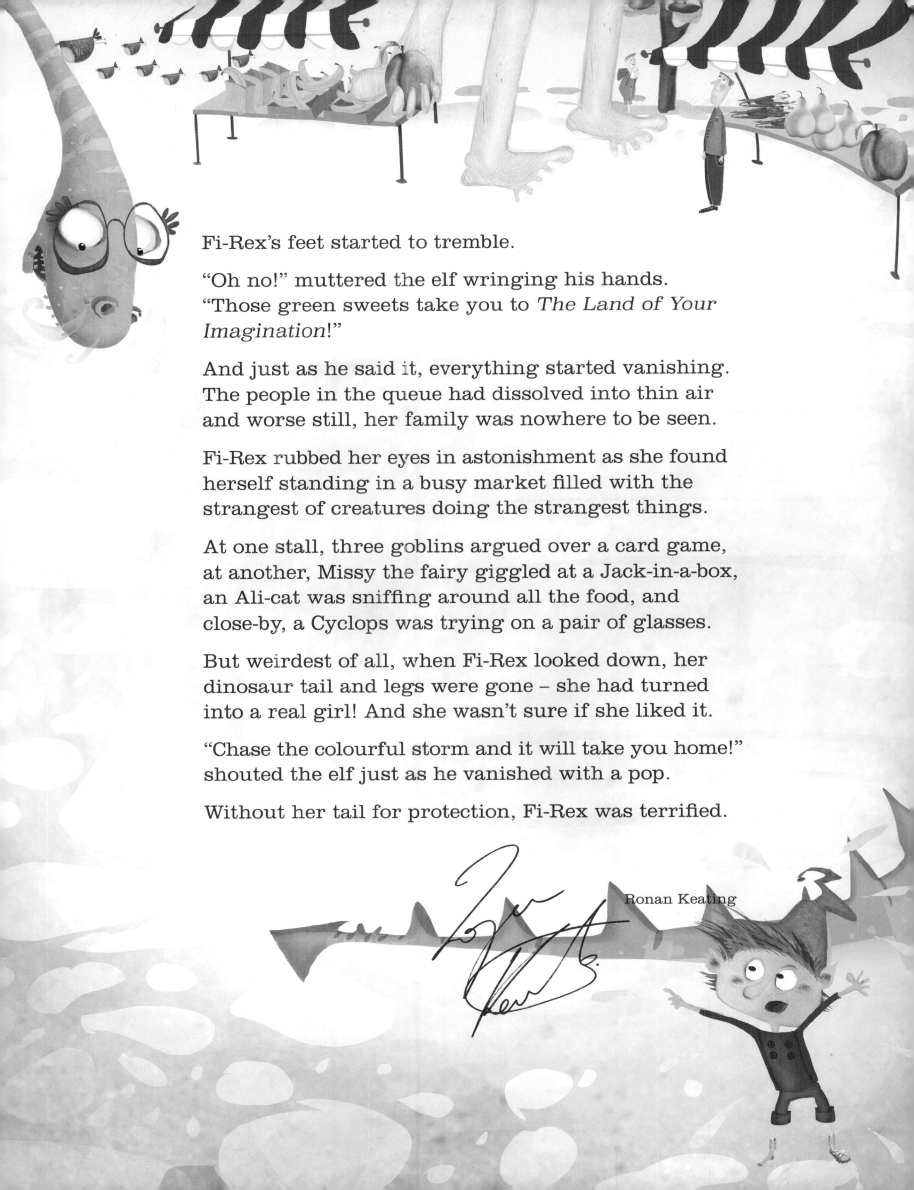

Fi-Rex's feet started to tremble.

"Oh no!" muttered the elf wringing his hands. "Those green sweets take you to *The Land of Your Imagination!*"

And just as he said it, everything started vanishing. The people in the queue had dissolved into thin air and worse still, her family was nowhere to be seen.

Fi-Rex rubbed her eyes in astonishment as she found herself standing in a busy market filled with the strangest of creatures doing the strangest things.

At one stall, three goblins argued over a card game, at another, Missy the fairy giggled at a Jack-in-a-box, an Ali-cat was sniffing around all the food, and close-by, a Cyclops was trying on a pair of glasses.

But weirdest of all, when Fi-Rex looked down, her dinosaur tail and legs were gone – she had turned into a real girl! And she wasn't sure if she liked it.

"Chase the colourful storm and it will take you home!" shouted the elf just as he vanished with a pop.

Without her tail for protection, Fi-Rex was terrified.

Ronan Keating

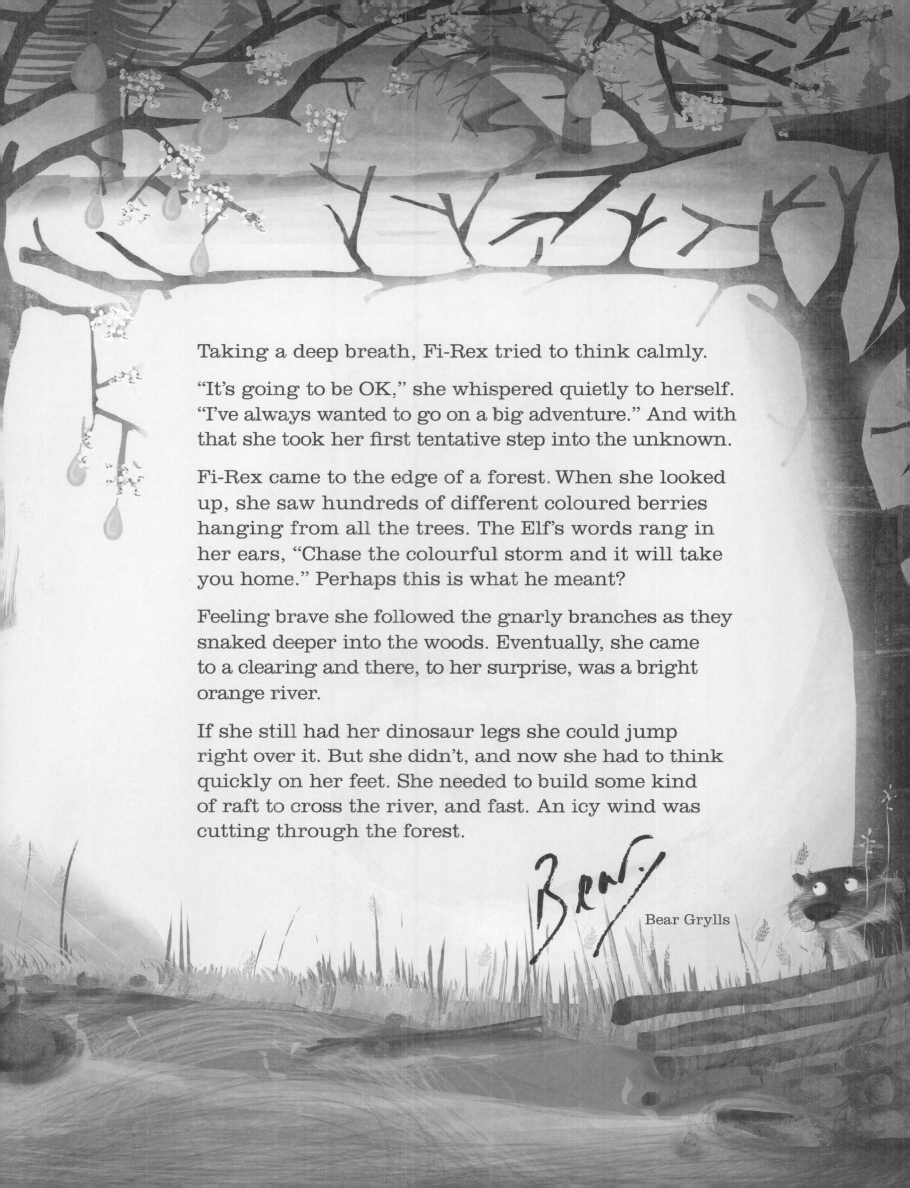

Taking a deep breath, Fi-Rex tried to think calmly.

"It's going to be OK," she whispered quietly to herself. "I've always wanted to go on a big adventure." And with that she took her first tentative step into the unknown.

Fi-Rex came to the edge of a forest. When she looked up, she saw hundreds of different coloured berries hanging from all the trees. The Elf's words rang in her ears, "Chase the colourful storm and it will take you home." Perhaps this is what he meant?

Feeling brave she followed the gnarly branches as they snaked deeper into the woods. Eventually, she came to a clearing and there, to her surprise, was a bright orange river.

If she still had her dinosaur legs she could jump right over it. But she didn't, and now she had to think quickly on her feet. She needed to build some kind of raft to cross the river, and fast. An icy wind was cutting through the forest.

Bear

Bear Grylls

It began to snow big heavy flakes, that settled like candy floss on her face.

"Whatcha looking for?" came a voice from the river. Fi-Rex looked deeply into the water, "Erm, I'm trying to cross you?" she said slowly, feeling silly.

Suddenly a small ripple appeared and up popped an otter's head. "How yer gonna do that then?" it asked chirpily, as Fi-Rex shrieked in surprise. "By making a raft out of sticks?" she said scrambling to her feet. "Well that won't work," said the otter hauling himself onto the riverbank. "We used them all for our den. You want to get up that tree and use that T-shirt of yours like a kite. I saw someone do it last week and it worked a treat."

Fi-Rex looked at the tall tree doubtfully but it was her only option. Up she climbed. "Here I go…" she said as she spread the sleeves of her top. They shone like gossamer wings as a huge gust of wind whooshed her over the river.

"I'm sailing!" Fi-Rex squealed with delight as she landed gracefully, like an angel, on top of a stripy circus tent. "Oh no," said Fi-Rex trying hard not to cry. "Which way is home?"

"I'll give you a clue!" said a booming voice from behind a tree, "but first of all you'll have to perform a trick!"

Penny Lancaster and Rod Stewart

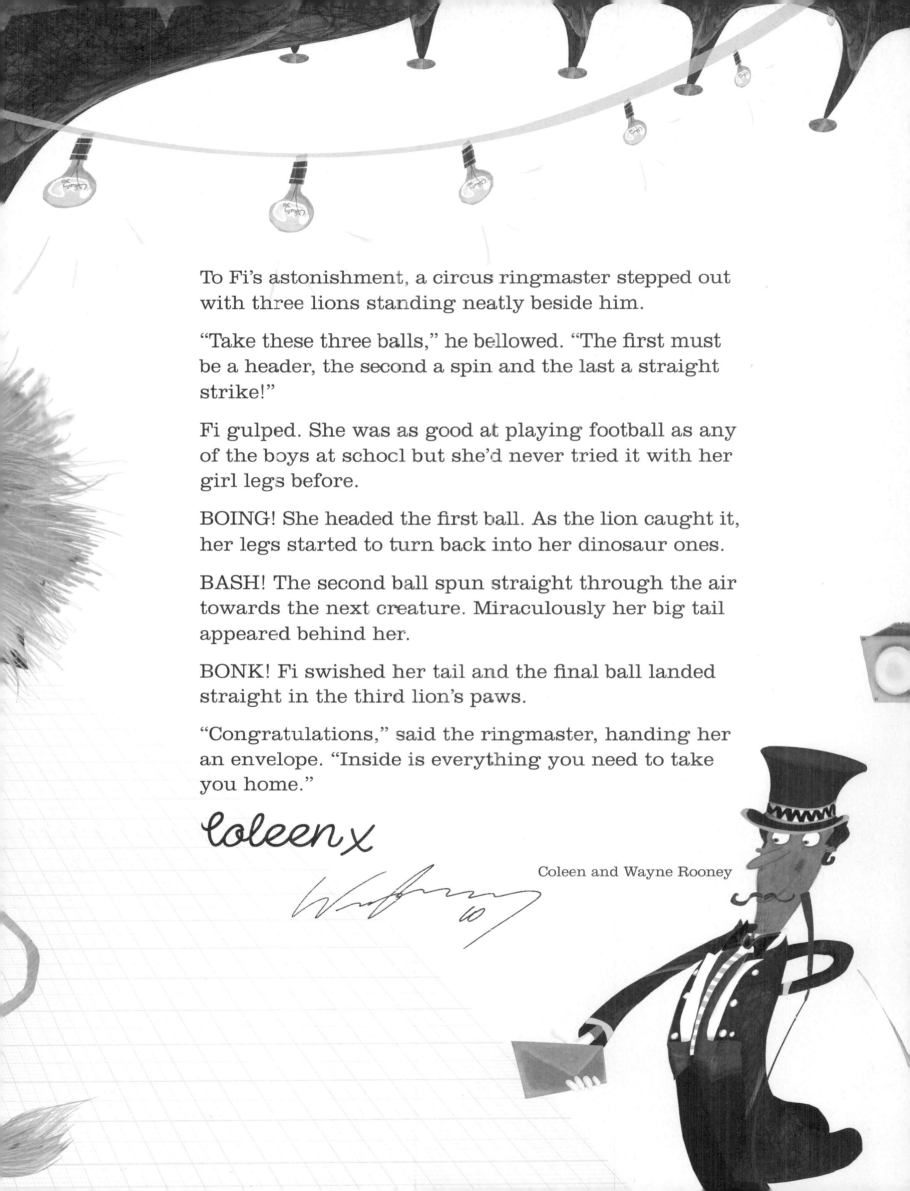

To Fi's astonishment, a circus ringmaster stepped out with three lions standing neatly beside him.

"Take these three balls," he bellowed. "The first must be a header, the second a spin and the last a straight strike!"

Fi gulped. She was as good at playing football as any of the boys at school but she'd never tried it with her girl legs before.

BOING! She headed the first ball. As the lion caught it, her legs started to turn back into her dinosaur ones.

BASH! The second ball spun straight through the air towards the next creature. Miraculously her big tail appeared behind her.

BONK! Fi swished her tail and the final ball landed straight in the third lion's paws.

"Congratulations," said the ringmaster, handing her an envelope. "Inside is everything you need to take you home."

Coleen x

Coleen and Wayne Rooney

TAKE ME HOME!

"To get back home, where it's nice and warm,
watch your step and stay out of the storm!
Only if you choose the right way will you
be home by the end of the day."

Ro ooar!

spot the

Home Farm

Way home

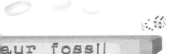

aur fossil

Phew! Finally she would be going back to her family.

Before opening the envelope she took a moment to think of all the wonderful things that would be waiting for her back home.

The warm heartfelt cuddles from Mum and Dad, hot chocolate with marshmallows before bedtime and her favourite board game of *Spot the Dinosaur Fossil* – because she always wins! Fi-Rex had even started to miss Max and his horrible habit of picking bogeys.

Ripping open the envelope she could hardly contain her excitement.

Inside was a piece of golden paper with a riddle written on it.

'To get back home, where it's nice and warm, watch your step and stay out of the storm! Only if you choose the right way, will you be home by the end of the day.'

Love

Denise Van Outen

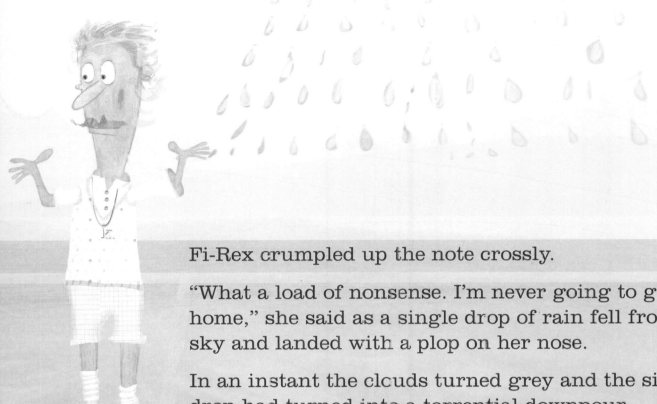

Fi-Rex crumpled up the note crossly.

"What a load of nonsense. I'm never going to get home," she said as a single drop of rain fell from the sky and landed with a plop on her nose.

In an instant the clouds turned grey and the single drop had turned into a torrential downpour.

"Well this just won't do at all!" came a voice behind her. Fi-Rex turned round to see a small man dressed all in white.

"I'm sorry but what won't do?" Fi asked, confused.

"Well the rain of course! With all this water we won't be able to play the game shall we my dear?!"

"What game?" Fi-Rex asked, "and who ARE you?"

"Well!" he replied indignantly, "I'm the umpire of course!"

Andy Murray

Andy Murray

donkey!

Don't show
Keith
your teeth

Zzzzz

"The umpire?" said Fi-Rex.

"Yes, the game we're about to play is soon to become an actual sporting event in the next Olympics."

"My name is Keith, Keith Lemon. I'm here to make your brother's seventh birfday party the best party ever, and the game is called *Don't Show Keith Your Teeth*."

The game was a word association game. "You mustn't laugh, pause or repeat a word but most of all you mustn't show Keith your teeth," he explained.

"OK, Fi-Rex. First you will be playing against this banana boy."

His name was Barry and like Fi-Rex he was half-human. The rest of him was banana!

Barry became half fruit when he was hit over the head one day in the school playground by a radioactive banana. A scientist had chucked it over the wall after trying to invent fruit that could walk to the supermarket by itself.

Keith stood between Fi-Rex and Barry the Banana and started the first round of the game.

"OK. The word I'm going to give you is... donkey," said Keith.

Keith Lemon

banana

farm

"Farm!" shouted Fi-Rex quickly. "Banana!" replied Barry.

"That's fifty bonus points to you!" said Keith excitedly patting the banana on the back. "You're making this up as you go along aren't you?" Fi-Rex said to Keith, feeling very annoyed.

"No, I'm not – the winner is Barry the Banana!" he shouted triumphantly, handing the banana a shiny gold medal.

Barry was so happy he slipped over his banana skin body. "I want a rematch!" Fi-Rex said. "Actually... I just want to go home."

"Well why didn't you say so?" Keith said kindly. "All you have to do is go to the top of the mountain and dive into the lake!" "What mountain?" Fi-Rex asked. As she did so, a snowy peak appeared on the horizon. "But how...?"

Fi-Rex turned to see Keith vanishing as quickly as he'd appeared in the first place. "Good luck little Dino girl!" he waved.

"Can I come with you?" asked Barry the Banana as Fi-Rex helped him up off the floor. "As long as you don't do any more splits!" she said as they headed up the mountain together.

Tom Daley

Way home

As they neared the peak, Fi-Rex could hear an instrument being tuned. "What's that noise?" asked Barry. "It sounds like an orchestra," said Fi-Rex. "And I think it's coming from behind those bushes."

"I wouldn't disturb that lot if I were you," a voice nearby squeaked. "Who said that?" asked Fi-Rex.

They looked down to see a beetle looking up at them. "They're always at it. Like eight days a week."

"Who are they?" asked Fi-Rex peering down at him. "The frogs, of course," the beetle replied. "Give us a lift up and I'll show you, but you have to be quiet."

Peeking through the leaves they could see hundreds of frogs, tightly packed around the edge of a lake. "They always stand together you see. It's better for the singing."

Suddenly a large, fat frog holding a baton let out a huge croak. It was so loud it made Barry the Banana slip over again and as Fi-Rex tried to save him, they both tumbled out of the bushes and landed with a plop on a lily pad.

"Oh, are you here for the concert?" asked the conductor, spinning round.

Sir Paul McCartney

"Of course we are!" Fi-Rex replied. "It feels like we've been queuing for hours!" "Have we?" asked Barry.

They sat down as the conductor tapped his baton and the band started playing their instruments. In the middle of the pond a large lily flower opened and four frogs jumped out singing and dancing as the huge crowd let out croaks of delight. "Who are they?" Fi-Rex asked.

"They're POND DIRECTION!!!!" screamed a frog, hopping up and down. "I've got all their albums and I love *That's What Makes Your Croak So Full.*" "Never heard of them," said Fi-Rex. "They're very good," said Barry. "Harry, Louis, Niall and Liam are my favourites." "That's all of them," snorted Fi-Rex. "I know!" Barry beamed.

Fi-Rex watched as the band jumped and danced and sang. At the end they raised their hands to silence the excited crowd. "Are we all having fun?" they asked. Croaks erupted in response. "We are Pond Direction and we need one of you up here to help us!" All the frogs hopped up and down, waving their hands to get their attention. "She'll do it!" shouted Barry the Banana.

Pond Direction looked over to an embarrassed Fi-Rex. "Don't mind him," she said. "I'm not here to sing – I'm just here to get home." "Well if you help us, we'll help you," Harry said, taking her hand and pulling her onto the lily pad.

One Direction

"Well, you don't see that every day," said a shrill voice above the hushed crowd. It was Gary, one of three ducks from a group called Quack That, who had been sunning themselves on a nearby riverbank. They were known as the quiz champions of the forest.

"What's that then?" quacked Howard ruffling his feathers. "Don't look up," said Gary mischievously. "Let's make it a game!" "Brilliant idea," quacked Mark and Howard in unison. They loved a quiz!

"Is it a big metal flying object with loads of humans flying through the sky?" asked Howard. "No, as if," laughed Gary. "Is it a big metal object with loads of humans inside driving through the grass?" asked Mark. "No! You're way off. What's green, has two arms, two legs, dark hair and a huge green tail?" asked Gary.

Mark and Howard closed their eyes and thought really long and hard, and then as if by magic, said, "Is it a half-girl, half-dinosaur called Fi-Rex riding on a lily pad with Harry from Pond Direction?" "How did you guess that?!" exclaimed Gary. "Because we're the quiz champions!" and all three did a high-wing! "Quack That!"

"Oh dear, and it locks like they might need our help," said Gary.

Take That

Right in the middle of the water, Fi-Rex and Harry the frog were clinging frantically onto a lily pad which was spinning out of control. "Help!" cried Fi-Rex holding on for dear life.

Gary swooped over. "What's going on?" he asked as he landed beside them. "This chivalrous frog has been trying to swim me back home, but we don't seem to be going anywhere," sniffed Fi-Rex. "I'm just desperate to get home for my brother's birthday," she gulped.

"Say no more!" said Gary as he scooped up Fi-Rex and put her on his back. "It's not exactly a private jet but you'll be back for good before you know it!" And with that they soared into the sky.

"This is AMAZING!" screamed Fi-Rex. "I can see for miles!" Then suddenly a rainbow of colours started to appear over the horizon. "Is that the colourful storm that will take me home?" she asked excitedly.

Looking down, Fi-Rex could now make out a river below with hundreds of rainbow flying fish jumping in and out, their shimmering colours reflecting in the ripples. "It's a fish rave!" Gary announced as his wings swooped just inches above the water. "Help! I'm going to fall off!" Fi-Rex shouted as she lost her grip on Gary's neck.

"G'day. I'll take it from here," said the sweetest of voices. A small fairy took her trembling hand and they fluttered into the darkness. "Now close your eyes and count to three." "ONE, TWO…"

Kate Moss, Nick Grimshaw
and Annabelle Neilson

"Are you all right Fi?" It was Mum lifting her off the floor. "You fell off your chair as Max was blowing out his candles!"

Fi-Rex stood shakily on her dinosaur feet looking at the flickering glow on top of the birthday cake where a fairy stood holding a candle.

"Thanks for the card Fi," Max said to her. "But you could have put something cooler on it than a banana singing to frogs!" "Trust me, Barry IS cool," Fi-Rex said, looking at the cards, presents and decorations in the room.

There on the table was a fluffy toy lion, a ginormous jar of jelly beans in every colour, a book about otters and a duck-shaped party hooter. "How bizarre, maybe it was a dream after all?" she thought to herself.

She looked at her family lovingly. "What's the matter Fi?" asked her mother. "Nothing Mum. I was just thinking how lucky I am to have you all," she said. "Come on you, let's get to that theme park," Mum replied throwing Fi-Rex a coat, which she expertly caught with her tail.

Just as she closed the door, Fi-Rex took a moment to take one quick look around.

"Thanks for helping me guys, even if it wasn't real, I really had a great time." "You're very welcome," said a beetle, sitting on the window ledge. "That's what friends are for."

Kylie Minogue

Thank You!

We would like to thank all of the authors
of this book for their time and energy
(and bonkers stories) which they have given
for free.

To Julia Patton for her sensational
illustrations that she created from her
wooden shed.

To the Bright Agency, Bounce Marketing
and Sales and Grantham Book Services.

X

BBC Children in Need exists to make a positive change to the lives of disadvantaged children and young people across the UK. The Charity's vision is that every child in the UK has a safe, happy and secure childhood and the chance to reach their potential.

BBC Children in Need are currently supporting over 2,500 projects that are working with children facing a range of disadvantages for example, poverty and deprivation; children who have been the victims of abuse or neglect or disabled young people. Over a one-year period, 480,000 children and young people are reached by projects supported by BBC Children in Need.

For more information or BBC Children in Need visit: bbc.co.uk/pudsey